MINNIE MALONEY
& MACARONI

MARK ALAN STAMATY

The Dial Press · New York

Library of Congress Cataloging in Publication Data
Stamaty, Mark Alan. Minnie Maloney and macaroni.
Summary: Convinced by her sister in their childhood that buying
seven boxes of macaroni daily will prevent bad luck, Minnie,
now grown up, is not pleased to find out her sister was only fooling.
[1. Macaroni—Fiction. 2. Brothers and sisters—Fiction] I. Title.
PZ7.S7837Mi [E] 76-2281
ISBN 0-8037-5588-0 ISBN 0-8037-5589-9 lib. bdg.

For Mrs. Faber

When Minnie Maloney was a little girl, her big sister, Molly, told her a secret. "If a person buys seven boxes of macaroni every day, she will be protected from bad luck."

When Minnie grew up, she remembered her sister's advice and followed it faithfully.

Because her family never ate macaroni, she had to give it all away. Soon a small group of macaroni lovers began waiting for her every day. After a while they started the "Minnie Maloney Macaroni Club" and made special club T-shirts.

The macaroni giveaway continued for a long time, and everyone was happy. Everyone except Minnie's husband, Murray.

"This is ridiculous!" he often shouted when he saw the grocery bill. "We can't *afford* to buy all this macaroni that we never eat!"

"Would you rather have bad luck?" was Minnie's reply.

"No," said Murray, heaving a hopeless sigh.

And Minnie kept buying macaroni.

Then one day Murray put his foot down. "I'll have no more of this nonsense!" he shouted. "I don't care if we have bad luck from now until next year! If you don't stop buying macaroni, I will move to Iceland and become a hermit!"

Minnie did not want him to do that, so she promised to stop buying macaroni.

But she didn't stop worrying about what might happen.

The next day when she didn't buy any macaroni, the members of the macaroni club were disappointed, but they understood.

"We'll just have to buy our own," they said. "We appreciate all you've done for us. Without you, we never would have started our club."

They gave her a big cheer, which pleased her but didn't stop her worries.

"I just *know* something awful will happen," she said to herself as she walked home.

Then . . . it happened.

In her nervousness she tripped on a curb, broke the heel of her shoe, and dropped her grocery bag. By the time she picked up the remains of her groceries and hobbled home, her favorite television program was over.

"Oh, no! This is terrible!" she exclaimed. "What awful thing will happen next?"

Just then Murray came in from the yard and tripped over the bag of groceries that Minnie had left in the doorway while rushing to the television. His glasses fell off and broke to pieces.

"This is awful!" he said.

"You see what happens when I don't buy macaroni?" said Minnie.

"Yes," Murray groaned. "I guess you were right. You'd better buy some before we have any more bad luck."

The next day Minnie bought seven boxes of macaroni, and everything was fine and dandy.

Then one morning she got a letter from her sister, Molly, who lived far away, saying she was planning to come for a visit. Minnie had not seen Molly in a long time, so she was very excited when they met at the airport.

The next day Molly happened to go with her to the grocery. "Why are you buying so much macaroni?" she asked.

"*You* know!" said Minnie.

"No, I don't," Molly said.

"What do you mean? *You're* the one who told me about it!"

"What are you talking about?"

"Don't you remember?" said Minnie. "One day when we were little, you whispered to me that if a person buys seven boxes of macaroni once a day, she would be protected from bad luck."

"Oh, now I remember," said Molly, laughing. "I was only fooling." Then she laughed some more.

Minnie was very angry to find out she had been fooled, and she was about to punch Molly in the nose when she got a better idea. After Molly stopped laughing, Minnie paid the grocer for the macaroni.

"You mean you're still going to buy it?" said Molly.

"I sure am," said Minnie. "Maybe you *thought* you were fooling, but it really works."

Later, while her sister took a shower, Minnie told Murray how Molly had fooled them.

"I'll punch her in the nose for that!" shouted Murray.

But when Minnie told him her plan, he changed his mind.

After that, strange things began to happen to Molly. When she got out of the shower, her shoes were missing. No one could find them, so she borrowed a pair from Minnie. The next day she bought a new pair, but when she got home, Minnie had found her old shoes. So Molly returned her new ones to the store. That night, after her shower, her shoes were missing again.

The next morning at breakfast Murray slipped while serving Molly's tomato juice and spilled it all over her dress.

Later that day Molly bought some new shoes, only to find her old ones again when she got home. At dinner Minnie slipped while serving the pudding and spilled it all over Molly's blouse and skirt.

The next morning Molly woke up to find both pairs of shoes missing.

"I can't *stand* this!" said Molly. "I've been having so much bad luck! When will it ever stop?"

"Why don't you try buying seven boxes of macaroni every day?" said Minnie. "That would stop it."

"That's ridiculous!" said Molly.

However, at breakfast the next morning, when Murray slipped and spilled a pitcher of pancake syrup on Molly's bathrobe, she changed her mind.

"I've *had* it!" said Molly. "I'll try *anything!*"

With that she walked straight to the grocery and bought seven boxes of macaroni, and nothing bad happened for the rest of the day.

So Molly bought seven boxes of macaroni every day for the rest of her visit, and she didn't have any more bad luck.

"Thank you so much for telling me about macaroni," she said when they took her to the airport. "I'm going to buy seven boxes every day from now on."

"Don't thank us," said Minnie. "Remember, it was *your* idea."

So they said good-bye, and Molly got on the plane. Then Minnie looked at Murray, and they laughed and laughed.

And they never bought macaroni again.

Mark Alan Stamaty is the author-illustrator of *Who Needs Donuts?* (Dial), which was one of the Child Study Association Books of the Year in 1973, a Society of Illustrators Gold Medal Award winner in 1974, and a recipient of the Brooklyn Art Books for Children Citation in 1975. "Dazzling . . . " said *The New York Times.* "Of the hundreds of ingredients here, two of them are definitely doughnuts and love."

Mr. Stamaty lives in New York City, where he is presently at work on a new book about the search for a missing hippopotamus.

J